Murder by Copy

MOON'S LANDING COZY MYSTERY SERIES
BOOK THREE

SHELLEY WEISS

Murder by Copy

Chapter One

"WHAT DO YOU MEAN, SOMEONE BROKE INTO Moon's News?" Blanche stood inside her office glaring at her assistant, Roy Beaker, in disapproval. "And the first thing you did was report it to the sheriff instead of calling me?"

Roy Beaker held several files against his chest as though they would keep him safe from her wrath. "It seemed like the obvious thing to do!" he yelped, defending himself.

It was late at night, and Beaker had called Blanche frantic. He described what he had found when he arrived at Moon's News, the local newspaper for Moon's Landing. He explained the main door of the newspaper office was wide open, and the reception desk's computer was on the floor and in pieces.

Blanche had been with Mason and me when she got the call, so the three of us rushed straight here together.

"I'm not surprised this happened to you." Doris Gilbert righted a chair to sit down, a sly smile on her face. "I had told you your lack of a security system would bite you in the—"

Blanche spun in her direction. "What are you doing here, Doris?" She demanded as she raked a hand through her messy blonde hair. "You don't work here."

Doris held her phone, snapping a few photos of the office. The office was in complete disarray. Chairs had been overthrown, and file cabinets overturned. It looked as though someone had a wonderful time making a mess.

"You're lucky I was here," she stated as she tucked her phone inside her purse. "I'm the one who insisted Beaker call the sheriff. I told him; If you don't call the sheriff, I will. My readers will love to read all about this in the morning."

Blanche looked ready to launch herself across the room at Doris, and I thought it best to intervene. I stepped between them. "Why don't we look around and list what's missing?"

A loud bang irrupted from down the hall interrupted us. Mason was the first to move to investigate the noise.

I stood locked in place, unable to move, afraid of what or who might have made that noise. "What was that?"

Mason stood in the doorway leading out into the hall. "Someone's here." He stood with his back to me, and I noticed how his light blonde hair caught the overhead lighting, making it look nearly white.

"What? Who?" Doris jumped out of her chair, clutching her purse to her chest. "I won't stay here a second longer."

Beaker inched towards the main door. "Blanche, it would be best to wait for the sheriff outside." But he wasn't willing to leave without his boss and stood rooted near the door.

Blanche shook her head. "And let whoever it is rob me blind?" She stormed across the room, straight into her father's office, returning with a golf club.

"Blanche, what are you doing with that?" I rushed to her side to keep her from doing what I feared. "Don't even think about going down there. We don't know who that is."

"All of you wait here." Mason headed down the hallway. Blanche and I followed and made it as far as the doorway. We stood huddled as we observed Mason check to see what had made that noise. He had no weapon — nothing that would protect him from an assailant.

To the left of the door was a stairwell leading up to the roof, and I felt a chilly breeze glide down and move through my dark brown hair. I glanced up as a flyer flew down to me.

I snatched it before it flew by. "What is this?"

Blanche took the flyer from my hand and read it. Her blue eyes narrowed. "What is this doing out here? This leaflet is normally inside our Sunday Paper to advertise our online subscriptions. It shouldn't be out here."

"It came from upstairs," I explained, but Blanche didn't hear me; she was too busy running down the hallway to see where Mason had disappeared.

"I think I hear a police siren!" Beaker hollered over his shoulder as he ran out of the building.

I don't know what compelled me, but I headed up the stairs leading to the rooftop. The door swung with the wind. I grabbed the handle as I reached the top of the stairs and peered outside.

I had forgotten Moon's News had a bird aviary for the messenger pigeons they kept on the roof. Blanche's dad, Fred, loved them, although I didn't think they were used to carry messages anymore.

The pigeons cooed loudly as they hopped around their aviaries frightfully. Something had them rattled.

I took one step forward but paused.

I wasn't out here alone.

An angry female voice bellowed across the rooftop. "I don't care what it takes. I won't stand for it!"

"Now listen here," a man roared back. "We are going to do this my way. Unless you want everyone to know—"

A gunshot rang out, and I ducked behind an aviary for protection.

Was that a gunshot? Was someone shot? Who was shot?

Booted footsteps rang near me, and I froze, hoping not to be seen. The steps paused on the other side of the aviary where I hid.

The birds began to dart and fly around the aviary, trying to escape. One bird was successful and landed on my back. I nearly screamed, but I clamped a hand over my mouth.

"Is someone here?" A woman's crisp voice demanded.

I peered around the corner of the aviary as she moved away, and I only caught sight of a burgundy boot as she darted around the corner.

"Birdie? Are you out here?" Mason stood in the doorway, sounding worried. He must have heard the gunshot.

"Birdie?" Blanche was near, too. "It sounded like a gunshot!"

I darted out of my hiding place and hurried to them. "She's still here," I cautioned.

"Who?" Mason stepped further onto the roof.

I pointed to the fire escape. "A woman! She must have gone that way." But I didn't run after her; instead, I headed in the direction I had heard the arguing. Worried about the man who had been shot. "Hello?" I asked.

"What happened?" Blanche was close behind me. I didn't know where Mason went. He might have gone after the woman.

The first thing I saw was a pair of legs protruding behind an aviary. "Oh, no." I hurried to his side to check on him. "Are you alright?"

"I'll call an ambulance," Blanche suggested as she removed her phone from a pocket, rushing away.

I knelt beside the man. He looked in his fifties, his salt-and-pepper grey hair loose around his scruffy face. A broken pair of tortoise-colored sunglasses lay next to him.

I glanced up to find Mason hurrying to my side. He knelt on the other side of the wounded man.

"He's dead." Mason notified, his voice dry.

I stood and shook my head in disbelief.

Blanche returned to my side. "Oh, no!" She drew a hand to her mouth. "That's our janitor! Kentucky Marv!"

"Kentucky Marv?" I asked, finding the name unusual.

"What was he doing up here?" Mason questioned as he searched Marv's pockets. "And why would anyone want him dead?"

"What are you doing, Mason?" Blanche inquired, her eyes narrowing in disapproval.

Mason stood as more police sirens ranged below us and smiled in my direction. "I've got good news for you, Birdie."

I thought maybe he had found something in Kentucky Marv's pockets. "What's the good news?"

"The good news is, you're not a murder suspect."

"What's the bad news?" I asked.

He pointed at Doris Gilbert standing in the doorway, cell phone in hand, and pointed right at us.

"She's going to scoop Blanche on the story."

Chapter Two

"WHAT ARE YOU DOING UP HERE?" BLANCHE marched over to Doris with her hands firmly on her hips. "Are you taking photos of my crime scene?"

Doris promptly deposited her phone into her bag and patted the curls of her blonde-grey hair. "Nothing wrong with taking a photo for my blog. You looked great standing there, slightly bewildered."

"Give me that," Blanche ordered, reaching for Doris's purse.

Doris stepped back, clutching her purse close to her chest, before running down the stairs to escape Blanche. I was about to follow Blanche to keep her from doing anything too drastic, but Mason called me over.

"There's something in Kentucky's hand." He declared as he was bent next to the body.

I crouched next to him, intrigued by what he could have found. "What is it?"

He began prying Kentucky Marv's fingers open to retrieve a scrap of paper.

I heard the noise of footsteps running up the stairs and knew we had little time.

Mason opened the palm, revealing a scrap of paper. The word 'Dire' and the initials T.D. were written on it. But what could this be about?

"What's going on out here?" Deputy Ben Griffins inquired as he stood in the doorway. "Birdie? Mason? What have you got over there?"

Mason and I both stood. Mason quickly pocketed the note as we exchanged a glance.

"It's Kentucky Marv," I reported.

Deputy Griffin's eyes widened in surprise. He quickly went to see for himself, followed by Deputy Joe Murphy.

"Do you know him?" I asked, surprised by the concern I had caught in Deputy Griffins' eyes.

"Do I know him?" He repeated twice and then nodded. "Yes, I know him. That's the sheriff's cousin." Griffins spotted Mason and shook his hand. "Hey there, Mason. I tried to get tickets to the brewery's party next week, but they sold out. My fiancée has her heart set on going." He leaned in as he mumbled. "Any chance of getting a couple of tickets?"

Deputy Murphy hid a cough behind his hand, and I coyly smiled. The party Griffins wanted tickets to is the upcoming Midnight Gala at the Old Brewery.

"Sir," Murphy stated as he stepped forward. "Do you think we should radio the sheriff about this?" He held his radio in his hand as we awaited the order.

The sheriff! I glanced at Mason. I hoped not. He wouldn't want to see me so soon after what happened at the marina.

Griffins placed his hands on his belt and leaned back on his feet as he nodded. "Why don't you radio this in, but give Lomack a call first."

"Deputy Lomack?" I asked, curious about the need for

Lomack's involvement. I knew he wouldn't want to see me so soon, either.

Griffins nodded. "Lomack will help cushion the news." He took out his notepad and began questioning us about what had happened before he had arrived.

I told Griffins everything I had seen and heard, and he quietly listened and jotted down notes here and there. He then suggested Mason and I wait downstairs in case the sheriff had questions.

I stopped in the middle of the stairwell to turn back to Mason. "The sheriff is coming here," I stated with concern. "The same sheriff helping Lois Jones cover her tracks with the misdealings she's doing within the H.O.A."

Lois Jones is the President of my H.O.A. Mason, Blanche, and I had just recently discovered that she has had a hand in embezzling money from the Homeowners Association, but we can't prove it — at least not yet.

"The sheriff will be too busy with this case to cover anything for Lois," Mason claimed as he led the way downstairs. "Leaving her vulnerable for our investigation."

What has the sheriff already done for Lois? The thought sent chills up my arms and caused me to shiver.

"Are you alright?" Mason asked with concern.

I nodded and then became distracted as I caught sight of Blanche speaking with Doris.

Blanche was pointing at Doris's purse. "You have to delete any and all photos you took here," she ordered.

"What? Are you serious?" Doris challenged with a coy smile. "Isn't that the pot calling the kettle black?"

"What?" Blanche raised her eyebrows in bafflement. "What are you talking about?"

"You printed photos from the murder at the marina in your newspaper, even after Deputy Lomack didn't want you to." Doris was happy to point out.

"Blanche," I said as I hurried over. I didn't want Blanche to strangle Doris, although it was unlikely. However, the temptation might arise, and I wanted to avoid her arrest. I eyed the deputies in the lobby with concern. "I need to speak with you."

Blanche shot a sharp gaze in my direction. "Birdie now is not the time. Can't you see I'm—"

"You'll want to know about this," I pressed, turning her toward her office and giving her a light push. I needed to share Mason's clue with her, but I had to ensure Doris wouldn't hear a word.

Doris followed us. Mason stepped in front, speaking to her, but not before slipping me the note he had found. I ushered Blanche into her office and locked the door.

"Birdie, what is this all about?" She crossed her arms as she ordered me to explain myself. "Doris Gilbert won't beat me to this story."

I held the note up and pointed at it. "Mason found this in Kentucky Marv's hand," I confided.

Blanche swiftly reached for it, snatching it out of my fingers. "What is this?" She inquired as she read it. Her eyes grew large as she looked back at me and slowly smiled. "This is a clue."

I nodded. "Yes, but who is T.D.?"

She repeated the initials several times as she gave it some thought. Beaker knocked at the door before trying the handle. Unlocking the door, he stuck his head in and informed us the sheriff had requested our presence.

The sheriff must have grown impatient because he pushed past Beaker, shouting my name.

"Birdie Lopez, I have a mind to arrest you," Sheriff Newbaker roared. "What have you done?"

"Sheriff Newbaker," Blanche boomed. "I'm so sorry about Kentucky Marv."

"What happened here?" He demanded. "What have you wrapped Kentucky Marv in?"

I shook my head. "We don't know exactly what happened to him, but—"

He turned sharply to me. "I don't want to hear from you," he stated firmly before moving to Blanche. "I was told you heard an argument between Kentucky and some woman."

"I'm sorry, but I didn't hear the argument. That would be Birdie." Blanche tilted her head at me before moving behind her desk to take a seat.

Before departing, Beaker stood by the door, giving me a pained look. I'd rather he had remained, but at least I had Blanche. Newbaker stood in front of me. I had to look up to meet his glare, as he was a head taller than me.

"What happened?" He asked, or, rather, demanded.

I explained what I had witnessed in detail, but his skeptical gaze revealed disbelief. His following words confirmed my suspicions.

"It makes little sense why Kentucky Marv would have been on the roof with those birds," he replied, flabbergasted. "He hates birds. Flying rats is what he had called them."

A knock sounded at the door before Deputy Lomack stuck his head inside. "Everything alright in here?" He inquired. "I heard raised voices."

"No," Newbaker screeched. "But I have what I need." He pointed at Lomack. "Take care of this, will you?" He pushed past him.

Blanche called after him, but Newbaker didn't return. Lomack kept her from pursuing him by raising his hand. "He needs to be alone right now."

"I needed to speak to him about the case," Blanche stressed. She had rounded the corner of her desk, ready to charge out the door.

"Is there any more information you'd like to give him?" Lomack demanded. "If so, you can give it to me, and I'll relay it."

At that moment, I realized I hadn't mentioned the clue Mason had found. I reached for my pocket but remembered I had given the note to Blanche. "Deputy Lomack—"

She shook her head in disapproval. She had a way of reading me. Blanche swiftly ducked under his arm and left the office without a word. Lomack turned to me, his eyes serious.

"You should stay as far away from this case as possible," he advised.

"But I'm a witness," I pointed out.

Lomack closed the door; it was just him and me.

"What is this about?" I inquired.

He took a deep breath and grimaced. "It's a unique situation."

"I'm sure it is," I said. "Kentucky Marv was the Sheriff's cousin?"

He nodded. "I can advise you to stay out of this case, but

it won't help. But I want you to know this. Kentucky Marv wasn't just an ordinary janitor." Lomack leaned in close and muttered, "He had his hands in shady dealings."

"Shady dealings? I'm not surprised," I answered as I recalled the note we had found. "Would you know anyone with the initials T.D.?"

Just as Lomack was going to answer, the door to the office opened.

Beaker stuck his head inside. "Birdie," he began. "Blanche was just arrested. I have to go to the station."

"What?" I asked, surprised. "Why was she arrested?"

"She may have said something about Kentucky Marv, and the Sheriff may have taken it personally."

"What?" I repeated as I hurried out.

"She's sitting in the patrol car if you want to talk to her."

Lomack groaned heavily. "Don't worry, I'll have her released."

Chapter Four

Lomack kept his promise and quickly got Blanche out of the patrol car despite Newbaker's reluctance. I headed home to Butterscotch, my coonhound, and headed for bed.

Butterscotch and I were up early the following day and out the door before sunrise. Butterscotch took the lead as I followed her mindlessly as we made our way through the neighborhood lined with Victorian houses.

Before I had left Moon's News, Blanche had informed me that there were three people she knew with the initials T.D.: Tony Diggs, a former writer for the paper, Taddy Dixon, and Tatum Duhmal. Blanche didn't know Taddy Dixon because her father had been the one to handle all correspondence with her. Taddy Dixon had an advice column, and Tatum Duhmal was a delivery driver for the newspaper and was currently in Florida.

The name Dixon is familiar, and it reminded me of my Aunt Lula. Her surname was Dixon. But I didn't know a Taddy Dixon. Butterscotch pulled me out of my thoughts as she barked at me. I realized we had returned home and stood in the lane leading up to our house.

I inherited my aunt's three-story Victorian Manor and her dog, Butterscotch. Aunt Lula had loved this house, and it's been growing on me too. The house would be perfect if not for the H.O.A., but nothing is perfect.

A shadow moved on my porch, causing me to gasp in surprise. Butterscotch made a friendly bark and wagged her tail as she trotted to the porch. It had to be someone Butterscotch knew, or she wouldn't act so nice.

"Hello?" I called out as we approached. Leaving the lights off was a mistake on my part.

"Birdie?" Lindsay Zimmer hurried down the porch steps. "It's me, Lindsay."

It felt good to see Lindsay away from the hospital. A car had nearly hit her while she was running, causing her to be admitted. "How are you feeling?" I asked as I gave her a quick hug.

"Could be better," she admitted, bending to greet Butterscotch. "Do you have a quick second? I've brought you some cupcakes." She held up an enclosed tray, holding the handle loosely. "I wasn't sure what you'd like, so I brought several."

I grinned and held out my hands for the tray. "I love cupcakes. Come inside. What are you doing up so early?" Because it was chilly, I lit the fireplace and sat across from her on an oversized chair. "I can make us some tea," I offered. "Although I'm sure it's nowhere near as good as what you make in your cafe."

"Tea sounds lovely," she retorted as she took off her coat and set it over the arm of the chair. "I'll help."

Lindsay followed me into the kitchen, and I grabbed the electric kettle. "I'm used to getting up early," she explained. "Early mornings are dedicated to making pastries and cakes at the cafe."

"I'm glad to see you out of the hospital," I said. "But what are you doing here?"

She removed two cups from the shelf and gave me a sheepish glance before focusing on the tea. She leaned against the counter and closed her eyes. "After all the trouble I had caused you, I thought I owed you an explanation. I haven't been entirely truthful."

I nearly dropped the tea leaves down the drain instead of the teapot infuser. Will she tell me what happened between Lois Jones and my Aunt Lula? I didn't say a word as I waited for her to speak. I could hear the water in the kettle heat as I waited for her to continue, but she was hesitant, so I prompted her by taking the cups she held in her hands.

Lindsay opened her eyes and looked straight at me. "I had helped Lois with her election campaign when she ran for a seat on the H.O.A.; it was a real eye-opener. I don't think she intended for me to learn what I had, and when she realized it, it was too late."

"What did you learn?" I asked.

"Lois had an excessive desire to win and would have by a landslide. But then we learned from Doris Gilbert that your aunt had decided to run against her — well, Lois knew how popular your aunt was in the community. She knew how much Lula was loved and respected."

I didn't know my aunt wanted a seat on the H.O.A.; she had never discussed it.

Butterscotch rubbed my hand with her nose before heading outside through the doggy door.

Lindsay poured the tea. "The sheriff visited your aunt. I heard about it when he came to speak with Lois. He informed her that Lula had withdrawn from the election."

"What?" My mind raced with worry as I became concerned about what had happened between my aunt and the sheriff. "Did the sheriff say what he had done or said to my aunt?"

Again, Lindsay shook her head. She crossed her arms and leaned back against the counter. "After the sheriff left, I confronted Lois and told her I would no longer help her with the campaign. But she promised she would help me."

"Help you with what?" I asked.

"Lois knew I wanted to open Sweeties Latte's, but I didn't have the capital... she promised to make sure I got it if I kept quiet. She has a friend at the bank." Lindsay turned squarely at me, her eyes locked with mine, tears filling them. "I'm so sorry, but things might have happened differently if I hadn't kept quiet."

I reached for Lindsay, wrapping my arms around her shoulders. "What happened to my Aunt Lula wasn't your fault."

"But because I kept quiet, Lois won the election, and now she's running this town as though she were its mayor."

"I'm sure the mayor would feel differently about that." I pulled away and grinned as the scent of chamomile filled the air. "The tea's ready."

Lindsay used her hand to wipe her eyes. "Oh, I almost forgot the other reason I came here."

I handed her a cup, sure that whatever the other reason could be would be nowhere near as important as what she had already told me. Picking a chocolate cupcake from Lindsay's tray, I called for Butterscotch by opening the back door.

"I almost forgot to tell you. Blanche mentioned you wanted to know the name of the man your aunt was dating. I was surprised you didn't know about him."

Stunned, I turned back to her. "Are you saying you know who he was?"

Lindsay took a sip of the tea. "Mmmm hmm," she began. "You know him too. It's Brent Lomack."

I nearly dropped my teacup. A splash of it landed on my fingers, causing me to wince. "Brent Lomack?" Had I heard right? "Deputy Lomack was dating my Aunt Lula?"

ONCE AGAIN, BUTTERSCOTCH AND I HEADED OUT for a quick turn around the block. We had a full day planned, which included returning to Moon's News to see what I could dig up on Taddy Dixon, Tony Diggs, and Tatum Duhmal. I was confident I could decipher the note's meaning and which one it was intended for.

What was dire? Had he predicted his murder?

As Butterscotch and I headed down the street, my neighbor Flora Moon called out to us. Flora, Mason's great-aunt, lives with her sister Petunia across the street in a grey Victorian.

"Dearie," Flora called, waving. "Oh, dearie!"

The Moon sisters were not the most pleasant, and I did my best to avoid them. "Good morning, Ms. Flora," I replied in greeting as Butterscotch and I crossed the street to her. "How are you?"

"It's about your dog," she declared as she pointed at Butterscotch. "She was out early this morning barking up a ruckus! And I need to know what you will do about it."

"What?" I asked, surprised. "I didn't hear Butterscotch. Are you sure you have it right?"

Butterscotch sat at attention, staring up at Flora, her head tilted at her in question.

Flora placed her hands on her hips with a very sharp look directed at Butterscotch. "I'm sure I have it right," she moaned. "See about your dog." She turned and headed right back into her house.

Butterscotch and I exchanged confused glances. "What is she talking about?" I asked.

Butterscotch raised an ear and gave me a side-eye before standing and tugging at her leash to get going. We made it through the rest of our walk without another run-in with one of the Moon sisters.

I had arranged for a cab service on my phone app, and I had just enough time to run upstairs, shower, and get ready before it arrived. It took me about twenty minutes, but I was heading out the door dressed in a fitted rose-colored blouse with a bow at the neck and capped sleeves. It was one of my favorite pieces I had picked up at an estate sale. I paired the blouse with a just-below-the-knee rose and white checkered 1940s skirt and white flats.

The cab was waiting outside, and I grabbed my 1940s vintage compact, tossed it inside a hand-beaded purse, and reached for my phone charging on the side table.

Butterscotch and I hurried into the waiting cab. I opened my purse to tuck my phone inside, but a pack of cigarettes stared at me. I grabbed the wrong bag in a hurry, meaning I didn't have my wallet! I removed a cigarette from the cartoon, fiddling with its weight between my fingers. But, determinedly, I tossed the cigarette back inside my purse and pulled out my compact to powder my nose.

I caught the cab driver eyeing me through the rearview

mirror. "You know," he stated kindly. "You resemble someone from another era."

Smiling, I thanked him. I couldn't help it; I loved the style of the 1930s and 40s.

Butterscotch sat with me in the back, and I rolled down the window so she could enjoy the fresh air. The drive into town was pleasant, with minimal traffic. In about twenty minutes, I caught sight of the Moon's News sign.

"Here's my stop," I announced as I pointed out the building.

Moon's News was a three-story building with a large sign posted on the roof in bright blue letters. I spotted Roy Beaker heading inside carrying a cardboard box. I called his name as we got out of the car.

"Birdie," he declared with a smile. "You're just in time for breakfast. Blanche had me pick up takeout." Butterscotch broke free from me and trotted to his side to say hello. "Hey there, Butter."

I peered into the box and saw bagels, various cream cheese containers, and coffee. I scooped up Butterscotch's leash. "What time did you and Blanche get to Moon's News?" I inquired as I held the door open for him.

Beaker smiled as he strode past. "We never left."

I choked in surprise. "Oh, I'm so sorry." We followed him through a maze of organized chaos as employees darted to and from Blanche's office.

Beaker shrugged. "I learned early on in my career here that I'd be working on Blanche's schedule and to keep an overnight bag in my office."

I nodded in agreement. "She gets laser-focused on projects, doesn't she?" I took the box from Beaker as he reached to answer a ringing phone.

When he finished the call, he rolled his eyes and cleared his throat. "I've been fielding calls about Kentucky Marv's murder all morning, thanks to Doris Gilbert's article. And I tell them all the same; you can read about it in the paper!"

I fished a bagel out of the box. "You sound more and more like Blanche every day!" I laughed as his face fell in disappointment. "Would you mind if I look at your archives? I want to discover Taddy Dixon's identity."

"Don't you know?" He asked, confused.

"No, I don't. I don't have a clue who Taddy Dixon could be," I said.

He removed two coffee cups and headed towards Blanche's office. "Why don't you look through the old man's — ahem, Mr. Pruitt's employee files." Beaker blushed.

I hid a smile behind my hand. "Do you know where he keeps the files?"

He nodded. "In his office. Here, I'll unlock the door for you."

Within moments, I settled into Henry Pruitt's office and reviewed his employee files. Butterscotch kept watch at the door. Not that it was necessary, but she appeared content.

I had all the employee files labeled under 'D' in my lap and quickly pulled free the one tagged Taddy Dixon. My jaw nearly dropped. My Aunt Lula was Taddy Dixon. Taddy Dixon was her pen name! Why didn't she ever tell me?

Before running out of the office searching for Blanche, I grabbed the files for Tony Diggs and Tatum Duhmel.

"Blanche," I shrieked as I hurried down the hall. "Taddy Dixon was my aunt!"

Blanche was in her office, and she wasn't alone.

"Aunt Lula was Taddy Dixon," I called out before realizing Deputy Lomack sat in front of her desk. He turned as I opened the door. I closed my mouth and stammered out an apology. Butterscotch rushed to him and landed her front paws on his lap. Lomack growled with such an attack and patted her head in a familiar greeting.

"What is this about?" Lomack asked after he calmed Butterscotch down. She pushed off his lap and sat down next to him.

"Deputy Lomack was asking me about last night," Blanche shared. She raised her eyebrow in surprise at what I had blurted out.

I had a few questions for Lomack. Why hadn't he told me he was the mystery man dating my aunt? "Deputy Lomack," I said as I gripped the door handle.

Lomack sat back in his chair, crossing his arms. "Blanche already told me you had found a note."

"Forget about the note," I said as I closed the door. "I

want to know why you never told me about your relationship with my aunt."

"It wasn't a secret," he said as he straightened up in his chair.

"But wasn't it?" Blanche inquired. "Birdie and I didn't know about it."

"It was my business," he growled. "And it doesn't concern either of you."

"But doesn't it?" I asked. "Or were you afraid of becoming a suspect?"

Rising from his chair, he directed his finger towards me. "We know who caused your aunt's death. And he's sitting in jail awaiting trial."

Butterscotch pawed at me with her front paw. She didn't like to see me upset. "That doesn't explain why you didn't tell me," I firmly stated.

"I only knew you through your aunt, and she talked about you as though you were perfect. And in my line of work, I know no one is perfect. But you know about us now, and how does knowing about it change what happened?"

What kind of answer was that? Blanche must have seen the fury in my eyes as she stood behind her desk. "Deputy Lomack, what about the notes left for us? Was that you?"

Lomack took a moment to answer. "Yes."

"That was you?" I asked, floored.

Blanche sat back down, looking quite pleased with herself. "I had a strong hunch it might have been you. I've seen your writing in your police reports."

Why didn't Blanche share that suspicion with me? I didn't get to ask because Beaker knocked on the door, almost hitting me in the back when he opened it, forcing me to move.

"Blanche," Beaker began. "The bank is on line two." He pointed at the phone, looking rather uncomfortable.

Lomack rose and headed out the door, and I pursued him. "Not so fast," I announced.

Lomack turned back to me. We both stood outside the office door, and Beaker had to move between us to return to the front desk. He picked up the line, and I was sure he was eavesdropping on Blanche's call.

"I have work," Lomack claimed. "What more do you need to know?"

"I want to know why you dropped clues for me with those notes," I said as I crossed my arms. "And I want to know why my aunt never told me about the two of you."

He closed his eyes and shook his head. "I don't know why your aunt never told you. I can't answer for her. But I left those notes ...because I loved your aunt."

Chapter Seven

After speaking with Lomack, Butterscotch and I headed up to the rooftop. I wanted to check for missed clues, but I also needed fresh air to clear my head.

Butterscotch moved freely around the roof as I stood before an aviary, watching the pigeons move around and listening to them cooing. Up here, it was pretty calming. I could understand why Henry Pruitt enjoyed this.

Butterscotch drew me out of my stupor as she growled. It was low and soft but rose in pitch. "Butterscotch? Come here," I called, but she wouldn't budge. She stood in front of an aviary at the other end of the roof. I knew she wasn't growling at the birds. It had to be someone.

I had an eerie sensation that we were not up here alone. "Come here," I ordered. I didn't want her to get harmed by whatever it was. Quickly, I moved to her side to find out who or what had Butterscotch's attention.

A woman in a tan suit emerged from behind the aviary. She had a leopard scarf covering everything but her eyes, hidden behind a pair of dark sunglasses. She pushed past me, and I tripped over Butterscotch, who darted at the woman.

"Butterscotch, no!" I yelled as I tried to regain my feet. "Come here."

Pigeons began flying out of their aviary, swirling around me. Butterscotch stopped at the door. She had no choice, as that woman slammed the door shut, blocking her from pursuing her.

I raced to the door, turned the knob, and pulled it open to chase the woman. I couldn't let her get away. What was she doing here? Was she the murderer I had seen last night?

As Butterscotch and I darted down the stairs, Beaker ran up them, and we nearly knocked right into each other. "Beaker," I shrieked in distress. "Just now, did you see a woman running down these stairs?"

"What?" He asked, confused, as he shook his head. "No. I was going up to look for you. Blanche needs to speak with you."

Butterscotch ran past him, still in pursuit of the woman. "I can't let her get away," I announced as I ran past. I caught up with Butterscotch, or, rather, she returned to me, but she wasn't empty-handed. Clutched in her teeth was the leopard scarf. She must have yanked it free of that woman, or it came off on its own. I took the scarf from her and returned to Beaker.

"Do you know who this belongs to?" I pleaded, hoping he did.

"Never seen it," he replied.

"Do you have security cameras?" Indeed, there are cameras around here, but I suddenly remembered Blanche telling the deputies last night that she had disabled the cameras to cut down on costs.

Again, he shook his head. "We had to scale back due to budget cuts."

I couldn't believe it.

"Blanche is trying to save money where she can so she won't have to cut staff," he revealed.

"But on security cameras?" How much could they be? But again, the realization hit me hard about how much the paper was struggling and her and her father's desperate situation. Did Beaker know her father is in hospice and trying to sell the paper?

Blanche had assured me that outside of his doctor and nurse, no one knew — well, Mason knew. Henry Pruitt had approached Mason with an offer to buy the paper. I didn't know if Mason had decided to purchase the paper yet or if Blanche had convinced her father not to sell. Could that be the reason for the phone call with the bank?

"Is Blanche still in her office?" I inquired as I headed for it.

"I believe she's heading out to the bank," he said.

"Let's go, Butterscotch," I called as we raced to find Blanche. "Maybe we can catch her before she leaves."

Blanche was easy to find. She was turning around the hall, and we nearly collided.

"Birdie," she hollered. "I've been looking for you." She held up her phone. I could see an article with the tagline, Murder Most Fowl! By Doris Gilbert. "Do you see what she's done?"

"But you already got your article out this morning," I pointed out.

Blanche held her cell phone closer to my face; missing the photo was impossible. "But she posted photos of us looking like fools."

I held the phone to see it clearly, and what a sight it was. I wanted to laugh but knew it would only anger her further. In the photo, Blanche was pointing directly at the camera with her jaw hanging open in anger, and I was bent over with my butt up in the air, while Butterscotch was darting off camera so only her hind legs were in the shot.

Blanche snatched her phone from my hands. "I can't go to the bank with this out in circulation," she mumbled. "We look like idiots!"

Beaker placed his hand on her shoulder. "I'm sure the loan officer is not reading old Doris Gilbert's blog." He took hold of her other shoulder, turning her to him. "You are going to go into that loan office, and you are going to look 'em right in the eyes and say, I'm Blanche Pruitt, and I deserve this loan."

Blanche looked at me for support. "Birdie..." She had the look of defeat in her eyes, and it pained me to see it there.

"You'll be okay," I assured her, guiding her from the hallway to the lobby. "What do you care what photo Doris took? You are more than a photo." But my words did not have the desired effect. She still had the look of defeat on her face. "Do you want us to go with you? We can wait outside?"

She shook her head. "No, I can handle it," she answered, determined.

Beaker handed her a briefcase and pushed her out the door. "Everything you need is in here. I got it all color-coded for you."

Butterscotch barked encouragingly, and we watched as she hurried to her car. "I'm so nervous for her," I announced.

"She's going to be fine," he assured. "She's meeting with Vivian Dupont. Vivian is an old friend of Henry Pruitt's, so how bad could the meeting go? I've got to run," he stated as he hurried off. "This paper will not run itself."

Chapter Eight

IT WAS NEARING TWO P.M. AS BUTTERSCOTCH, AND I headed over to *Sweeties Latte's*, and luckily, it wasn't as busy as it usually was at this time of day. Lindsay was cleaning up the table as we walked inside. She waved at us and showed she'd only be a minute by holding her index finger in the air as she neared a table full of customers with an anxious look.

Butterscotch and I headed to the dessert bar, patiently waiting for Lindsay, who appeared to be the only employee working today.

"Do you have help today?" I asked as she hurried over to the counter. She placed the used dishes on the counter behind her and smiled at me.

"I was supposed to," she stated, brushing her hair behind her ear. "But a couple of my girls called in sick." She leaned forward and whispered, "I think it has to do with what Doris Gilbert wrote in her blog this morning. Everyone's afraid of a murderer running loose around town."

I nodded. "I read it too. Blanche is upset about it, but I think for different reasons."

"All these murders. It was never like this before..." Lindsay said, wiping the counter. "All day, my customers have been asking if I know anything. They want to know what will happen next — who will be next."

"Moon's Landing used to be a quiet town," I said. "I'm sure Lomack will have someone in custody."

"Have you heard anything?" she asked, hopeful. "What has he said about it?"

"Did you know Kentucky Marv?"

She nodded. "Of course. He would come in here before closing to pick up his order. His standing order was a small coffee with cinnamon and a pecan muffin."

The bell at the door rang, causing us both to turn. Lomack and Joe Murphy walked inside, both dressed in uniform. It seemed they were always working. I returned to Lindsay to ask her a quick question before they approached the counter. "Any idea why someone would harm Kentucky Marv?"

"Not a clue. I'm sorry, I wish I could be more help," she glanced over my shoulder and back at me. "Lomack," she confided, warning me he was near.

"Hello there, Ms. Lopez, Ms. Zimmer," he said with a slight smile. He glanced at me and continued, "Don't you ever take a day off?"

"I was wondering the same about you," I sighed.

"Butterscotch," Joe squatted down to pet her. "Do you see something you'd like?" He pointed at the display window.

"Have you found anything out about Kentucky Marv?" I asked, but I knew he wouldn't share them with me if he did. I had just seen him at Moon's News, so I didn't think he'd have anything new, but it was worth the question. "Any comments for the paper?"

Lomack gave me a curious look before turning to Lindsay to order a large black coffee, no cream, no sugar. I couldn't help but make a face of disapproval.

"What?" He asked.

"That's your order?" I asked, disappointed.

"It's what I always order," he handed cash over to Lindsay and gave her a broad smile.

"You ordered a black coffee — your coffee has no soul, no character, nothing, just bleakness."

Joe began chuckling while Lomack stood unamused with my statement. Lindsay poured a cup of black coffee and handed it to him. "Here you go," she said.

He held off before accepting the cup. "Any idea when you'll start making those turtle things?"

"The turtle fudge?" She asked with a raised eyebrow.

He nodded. "That's the one."

"What about my question?" I reminded.

"About Kentucky Marv?" He turned back to me with a look of sharp disproval. "I've got nothing for you. No comment. And that's my official word."

But I had another question for him, one I had been thinking about for a while. "Can you tell me why his name was Kentucky Marv? Is he from Kentucky?"

Joe was quick to clarify. "It's quite simple," he said. "He's in a bowling league, and that's his moniker."

Lomack shook his head in disagreement. "That's not the reason."

"Uh." Joe looked skyward as he gave it some thought. "That's what I heard from—"

"What was the reason?" I asked.

Lindsay handed Joe his drink. "Here you go, your usual. An iced blend with two shots and no whip."

With that, they both turned, leaving me without an answer. I spotted Doris Gilbert eyeing us from a corner table. What was she doing here? How long has she been there, lurking?

I didn't need to wonder for long. Doris got up from her

table and hurried over. "I couldn't help but overhear your conversation with Deputy Lomack. It's a shame he wasn't much help to you, but I might have learned a thing or two about the case." She grinned coyly. "You're welcome to read about the case updates on my blog." She thanked Lindsay for her hospitality before leaving.

* * *

Since we were still in town, I looked up Tony Diggs. According to his employee file, he has an apartment in the city. Butterscotch and I walked the short way to his address. The apartment building was a two-story adobe structure with a gate leading into an enclosed courtyard.

Tony Diggs's apartment was up on the second floor. We climbed the iron stairs to the second floor and discovered his apartment at the walkway's end. Butterscotch sat at my side as I knocked on the door and waited.

Carefully, I peered in through the window beside the door; inside was a small living area with a sofa and a TV. On the off chance he was home, I knocked once more.

"Looks like he's not here," I said to Butterscotch, who stood at the sound of my voice. "Let's get home, shall we?"

While leaving, a woman stepped out from the neighboring apartment. "Hello?" She asked. "Can I help you?"

"Hi," I said as we stopped at her door. "Does Tony Diggs live here? Do you know if he's home?"

She tilted her head as she gave it some thought. "Yeah, but I haven't seen him in a few days. He mentioned leaving town, and that was the last I saw him."

"Did he say where he was going?"

"He said he got a job in the Bay Area," she leaned against the door jamb. "Do you want to leave a message in case I see him?"

"Sure, I'm Birdie Lopez from Moon's News and I just —"

She moved from the door as she interrupted me. "Moon's News? Do you work there? Isn't that where they found Kentucky Marv?"

Could she know something about Marv? "Do you know him?" I asked.

She leaned back and folded her arms as she gave it some thought. "I heard he ran into some trouble. The man liked to gamble."

"He did?" This was new! Maybe it would be helpful to look into it. "Do you know where he'd go to gamble?"

"He'd come by some nights to talk to Tony. These walls are so thin. Sometimes, I can hear them talking — I wasn't spying on them, but it was hard not to hear."

"What did they talk about?" I asked, anticipating she could tell me who Kentucky Marv was.

"Kentucky Marv was scared of someone. He owed his bookie a lot and thought Tony could help him. But Tony's broke! He's in his own hole." Her cell phone rang, and she glanced at it. "Hey, I got to take this, but good luck finding Kentucky Marv." She promptly stepped back inside and closed the door.

Who was Kentucky Marv's bookie? And where would I find him?

Chapter Nine

As promised, Butterscotch and I headed home, and after I had fed her, I sat in front of the fireplace with a cup of coffee and my cell phone and gave Deputy Joe Murphy a call.

He picked it up on the first ring. "Hello?" He asked. It sounded like he was eating because I could hear crunching coming from his end of the call.

"Hi Joe, it's Birdie," I said with a smile while keeping my fingers crossed. "Did I catch you at a good time?"

"Birdie! Sure, sure, what can I do for you?" He asked, clearing his throat.

I, too, cleared my throat. How should I ask him what he knew — if anything about the gambling circuit in Moon's Landing? After an awkward pause, I asked, "I heard that Kentucky Marv was in debt up to his eyeballs."

"You did?" He asked, surprised.

"Yes. I was hoping you would know where he would go to gamble?" I sat up in my chair as Joe was quiet.

He cleared his throat. It's a common occurrence tonight. "Is my answer going to be in Blanche's newspaper?"

"Oh, no, no, nothing like that," I assured.

"Well," he paused for a moment. "I really shouldn't be telling you any of this, but we have been having trouble with a local gambling ring. Lomack's efforts to find an informant have been unsuccessful. It's a tight circle."

"What if I told you I might know a guy?" I thought of Tony Diggs. "Although, I heard he may be in the Bay Area."

"What's his name?"

"Tony Diggs. He used to work for the paper."

"Tony Diggs," he slowly repeated the name. "Hold on a second... I know him."

I knew I shouldn't be surprised, but I was. "You do?" I could hear Joe typing and realized he must still be at work. "Are you at the station?"

"I'm always here," he said with a laugh. "Here we go. I have his file up on the computer." He grew quiet for a moment. "He's not in the Bay Area."

"He's not?"

"No, he was just released from our jail cells."

"What?" I mumbled into the phone.

"You say he knows about the circuit?" He asked, his tone serious.

"Yes, he knows all about the trouble Kentucky Marv got into. He knew Kentucky Marv was afraid of his bookie."

"Huh, I'll try to bring him in for questioning in the morning."

I heard keys brushing against a keyboard and grew excited about speaking to Tony Diggs. "Can I speak with him when you bring him in?" I asked.

He sighed. "I don't know. Lomack won't stand for it."

"He won't have to know about it." I crossed my fingers again and stood up, waiting for his answer. "I won't be long. It will be real quick!"

Joe cleared his throat. "Well, as long as you make it quick."

* * *

While cleaning dishes in the kitchen, a knock came at my front door. "Birdie?" Blanche called out in a panic. "Are you home?"

I hurried to the door. "What happened?" I asked. "Are you alright?"

"They denied me. They denied my loan," she stammered as she flew inside.

"What? Why?" I asked. Blanche had been prepared for the meeting and had an excellent credit history. Why did they deny her the loan to purchase Moon's News?

She sat in one of the oversized chairs by the fireplace and stared into the flames. I entered the kitchen, poured her an iced tea, and handed it to her. "Tell me what happened," I prompted as I sat across from her.

Blanche reached into her bag, removed a chocolate bar, and took a bite. She always ate chocolate when she was upset. "It started out going well; we talked about my ideas for growing the subscriptions — we discussed my business plan," she paused as she took another bite of chocolate. "I felt as though I held Vivian's interest because she kept smiling and nodding in agreement with me, but after I finished, she closed my portfolio and handed it back to me, saying there was no way she would approve my loan."

"Did she say why?" I asked, wanting an explanation.

Blanche nodded as she tossed the rest of the chocolate bar into her purse. "She said it was nothing personal, but she didn't believe I could run a newspaper."

"What?" I asked in shock as my jaw dropped to the floor.

"What am I going to do?" Blanche sat at the edge of her seat, her eyes wide with tears. "Do you know if Mason will buy the paper? If he doesn't, our newspaper must close its doors."

I shook my head. "I don't know, he didn't say." Although he had told me, I wasn't about to tell Blanche that Mason felt the same as Vivian!

Blanche became distracted as her cell phone rang and glanced at the screen. "It's my father's nurse. He knew I had an appointment with the bank today." She sent the call to voicemail and covered her eyes with her hands.

"What are you going to tell him?"

"He's going to be devastated," she choked. "When I told him I was meeting with Vivian Dupont, he got excited. He said they were good friends and was sure she'd approve the loan." Blanche grabbed her purse as she stood up. "I'd rather tell him in person."

I gave her a quick hug before walking her to the door. "I'm sure there's something we can do. This isn't the end."

She gave me a sideways smile. "Aunt Lula didn't leave you a fortune in gold, did she? I need time to process this. Don't worry, I will not give up."

Chapter Ten

It was after eight pm, and my phone rang as I was about to sit down for dinner. I hesitated briefly but quickly answered, thinking it might be Blanche. I rushed to retrieve it from the living room.

Recognizing the number as Mason's, I answered.

"Birdie, I need you at the brewery," he said, his voice tense.

"What is it?" I asked, what could this be about?

"You should come here," he insisted.

I quickly told him I would be on my way before disconnecting the call and ordering a taxi from my mobile app.

After about fifteen minutes, my taxi arrived, and I had Butterscotch in the cab with me on our way to the brewery, wondering what the mystery was all about.

"Are they having one of those fancy parties at the Brewery tonight?" My driver asked as he peered back at me through the rearview mirror.

I shook my head but smiled. "No, not that I know of."

He grinned back. "I haven't attended one of those parties but seen pictures of them."

Butterscotch stepped over my lap to get a better view from

my window. We were driving down Main Street, and she spotted a Great Dane being walked. It took me a moment to settle Butterscotch back down, and I was relieved to see the gates of the brewery.

What could Mason have to show me that warranted a late-night visit? Why couldn't he tell me over the phone?

I texted him to let him know I was near, and he told me to head to the warehouse. I passed the instructions to my driver.

Butterscotch barked as she spotted Mason waiting outside. He opened the door, and she excitedly jumped out, almost knocking him over.

"What is this all about?" I asked as I grabbed her leash.

"Come with me," he said as he led me inside. "I preferred not having this conversation on the phone. You'll soon understand why."

I followed him down a hallway and into a back employee break room. I detected the scent of a potent brew as I observed a couple of employees seated at a table drinking coffee.

"Have a seat," Mason said as he pulled out an empty chair. "You're going to want to hear what Boston Bob says."

"Boston Bob?" I asked with interest as I took a seat. Butterscotch circled the breakroom in search of mischief.

"Hello," the man seated across from me chirped, smiling. He wore a brown shirt with Moon's Brewery screen printed across the chest. The salt and pepper in his hair and the soft lines on his face gave him a friendly appearance. "I'm Boston Bob, and this," he pointed to his right where another employee sat. "This here is Wichita Willie."

"Wichita Willie?" I asked, confused by the name. "Why do they call you Wichita Willie? And you, Boston Bob? Are you from those areas?"

He chuckled, leaning his head far back and exploding with laughter. He rose in his chair and fixed his gaze on me. "How long have you been living in Moon's Landing?"

I shook my head. "Not long, but I've been visiting nearly all my life." Butterscotch returned to my side and bumped me with her head, ready to leave. "Just a minute," I said to her.

Boston Bob leaned forward. "A few things have happened in Moon's Landing since before your birth. In fact, since before many of us were born." he pointed at the man beside him. "Do you want to tell her the story?"

I grinned. "Story?" I eagerly asked, anticipating the secrets that he was about to reveal.

Mason shook his head. "Brace yourself. It's going to be a long one."

Wichita Willie spoke up, "No, no, it won't. Not if you tell it right."

I glanced between Wichita and Boston as I asked, "I'd like to hear it."

Boston Bob leaned forward in his chair with a sly look in his grey eyes. "It's how our Janitor's Union began," Boston Bob revealed.

"A Janitor's Union?" I asked.

"It's National," Wichita Willie added. "It formed in the 1920s when prohibition was at its peak."

"Whisky Moon wasn't alone in searching for a new start," stated Boston Bob.

"No. There were a handful of hobos in the area, too," Wichita explained.

"Hobos?" I asked, confused.

"Guys who moved from town to town but lived by a code of conduct," Wichita Willie explained. "An unbreakable code."

"Tell her," Boston Bob pressed. "Tell her how it started."

"Explain why she's here," Mason suggested, pulling out a chair and sitting at the table. Butterscotch hurried to his side, brushing his hand with her nose as she informed him she wanted attention. "Repeat to her what you told me," he instructed the two men while petting Butterscotch. "She doesn't need to hear the whole history."

Wichita Willie arched his graying brows with concern as he eyed Mason. "But she won't understand it unless she knows about the union and how it was made," Wichita Willie said with concern, his graying brows arching as he eyed Mason.

Leaving Mason, Butterscotch looped back to the break-room for a double-check.

"What is the code?" I asked them.

Boston Bob stood up and promptly closed the door and locked it. "Making sure no one walks in on us," he explained as he leaned against the door.

I turned back to Wichita Willie. "Go ahead," I implored as I leaned across the table, wanting to hear every word.

Wichita Willie cleared his throat. "I'll keep the explanation short," he began as he eyed Mason.

But Mason cut in. "The hobos in Moon's Landing formed a union, and today, nearly every union member can trace its roots back to one of the hobos who came to Moon's Landing looking for work."

Wichita Willie shook his head. "There's more to it, but yes."

"What does this have to do with Kentucky Marv?" I asked.

Boston Bob rushed to answer. "We are getting to that. You see, each of us has to live by a code. And if you don't, you must leave the union."

"Are you implying that someone murdered Kentucky Marv because he didn't adhere to the code?" I asked. What are they trying to tell me?

"He had a week tops to clear out his locker or pay his gambling debts," Wichita Willie said. "Kentucky Marv, he was in terrible debt. Everyone knew it because he asked each of us for cash."

"To pay his bookie?" I asked, knowing he had owed his bookie money.

"How did you hear about the bookie?" He asked, impressed. "But yes, he did, and he had to have it paid by the end of last week. But he flew the coop."

"He flew the coop?" I asked, confused.

"He flew the coop, he ran away," Boston Bob explained.

"But it looks like his bookie caught up to him," Wichita Willie explained. "Because why else—"

Butterscotch barked. She had made her way to the corner locker and sat on her hind legs as she gave it a curious look.

"Are you saying his bookie had him murdered?" I asked, focused on what Wichita Willie had just shared.

"He's dead, right?" Boston Bob asked while moving away from the door. "How else do you explain it?"

I turned back to Wichita Willie. "But murder?"

"I don't know if it was his bookie, but I was told to tell you what I knew, and now I have. More or less." Wichita Willie sat back in his chair.

"What is the bookie's name?" I asked.

"Kentucky Marv always used the same one—"

"Don't tell her," Boston Bob declared firmly. "What is the point of knowing? It will change nothing."

"The name's Rascal Ferret," Wichita Willie shared. "That's the name. But it won't do you any good to know it."

Mason stood up. "I know where we could find his bookie."

I quickly rose to my feet. "How?"

The other two eyed him curiously. "You're not taking her there, are you?" Boston Bob asked with concern.

"Take me where?"

Butterscotch released another bark, this one louder than the last. "What have you found there?" I asked her as I stood up to see what had her attention.

"Oh, you don't want any of that," Boston Bob said as he hurried over to her. "There's nothing for you in there."

"Butterscotch, come," I called. "Leave whatever that is alone."

But Mason walked over to the locker and tapped on it. The locker swung open, and out came a man wearing grey overalls with the name Moon's Whiskey printed across the back.

"Philadelphia Pete, what are you doing hiding in there?" Wichita Willie demanded in frustration.

Philadelphia Pete sat up and pointed at Wichita Willie. "The union will not be happy to hear about this." He ran out of the break room before anyone could stop him.

"I have to ask," I said as I put Butterscotch's leash back on. "Why was his name Kentucky Marv, but yours is Witchita Willie and you," I pointed at Boston Bob. "You are Boston Bob, and that—" I pointed at the door. "Was Philadelphia Pete. Shouldn't Kentucky have been Kentucky K—"

Boston Bob shook his head and laughed. "Kentucky Marv was always a bit different from the rest."

Witchia Willie took out his phone. "I need to get a hold of Philadelphia Pete before he does something he'll regret."

I didn't think I would get an answer about Kentucky Marv's name.

Chapter Eleven

MASON DROVE US TO THE 'MYSTERIOUS PLACE' AFTER we had dropped Butterscotch off at home, and I couldn't wait to get there. I imagined a speakeasy from the 1940s, but Mason brought us to a bowling alley called *Bootlegger's Bowl*.

On the roof sat a giant cowboy boot lit up in yellow marquee lights, and the dancing lights gave the impression that the boot was tilting over, spilling beer.

"What are we doing here?" I asked Mason, both confused and disappointed. "This doesn't look like the underbelly of Moon's Landing."

"Looks can be deceiving," he said as he parked the car. "Sorry to disappoint you, but Kentucky Marv spent most of his off time here."

"What do you suppose his bookie looks like?" I asked with a smile. "With a moniker like Rascal Ferret, it's got to be someone with a suspicious look. Maybe he has a twitchy mustache?"

I stepped out of the car and headed for the front door. Hanging over the door was a yellow banner that read: HOME OF MOON'S SHINER!

I winked at Mason. "Is this about you or your great-granddaddy?"

"Everybody's got a gimmick," he said with a shrug, holding the door open for me. "Let's head to the bar. I see Boston Bob."

Boston Bob and Wichita Willie chatted with a group wearing matching purple bowling shirts at one of the lanes.

Boston Bob broke away from the group when he spotted us and hurried over. "We were talking to some of our buddies. One of them told me Kentucky Marv always places his bets in the Janitor's Closet."

"The Janitor's Closet?" I asked.

"It's a private room," Mason pointed out.

"Let's go take a look," I said with excitement.

"Birdie, wait," Mason called after me, but I didn't wait. I didn't want them to stop me from investigating this lead.

It didn't take much footwork to make my way to the back. It was a reasonably tight space inside the bowling alley, but there was an upstairs. As I passed the stairs, I caught sight of a sign on a door to the right of the stairs that read Janitor's Closet and came to a halt.

"Wait a minute." Opening the door, I found nothing but cleaning supplies and a sink. "What is this?"

Mason stood behind me and said, "You're about to see." He then walked to the back wall, where a sink with a protruding plunger was located. I watched him move the plunger in the sink, turning the handle counterclockwise. He then knocked S.O.S. in Morse Code on the wall behind the sink.

"Welcome to the Society of Sanitation," Mason said as a secret door slid open.

"The Society of Sanitation?" I asked, confused.

Boston Bob filled me in. "It's the name of our union. This is where we hold our meetings."

"It's more than that," Mason argued. "It's a gambling hive."

I walked into the room, trying to catch sight of everything and everyone, but it was overwhelming. A circle bar sat in the middle of the room, and above the bar were electric scoreboards, flashing numbers. The room had more than a dozen bar tables, all occupied. More customers here than at the bowling alley!

I followed Mason through a group where a tall, slim man lifted his hand to his lips and 'hooted' right at me. Surprised, I had to stop and do a double-take. The group broke away and loosely encircled me.

"Are you lost?" a woman asked, nearly breaking out into a laugh.

"No." I glanced for Mason, but the thick crowd swallowed him up.

"Who's this girl?" The man to my left shook his head. I caught sight of a black mini notebook in his hand before he slid it away into his pocket.

I took a chance — or rather, a gamble. I moved close to the man and whispered, "You wouldn't be Rascal Ferret, would you?"

His dark eyes grew wide as he growled in discomfort. Oh no, did I do something wrong?

"Excuse me, *Miss?* But what did you ask me?" His eyes stared at me with dark intensity. I stepped back and right into a blonde woman smoking a cigarette.

"Watch it," she cracked, flicking ash on me.

I wiped down my dress as a redheaded woman to my right stepped forward. "Molly, I don't think she realizes she made a big mistake." Her smile grew wider as though she enjoyed watching me squirm. And I was!

"I'm sorry," I said. "I didn't mean—"

Mason and Boston Bob rushed to my side.

"There you are," Mason said, his eyes on me.

"She asked me if I'm Rascal Ferret." The bearded man said with disdain as he pointed at me. "What is she doing asking me if I'm Rascal Ferret?" His eyes bore down on me.

Mason took a step forward, protecting me with his body. "Clive Malone?" He asked.

"What?" He stuttered, caught off guard. "Do you know me?"

"You work at the brewery." Mason took a step forward. His broad shoulders blocked my view. I wanted so much to move past him to see the look on the other man's face, but all I could hear was the sudden tremble in his voice.

"Yes, I do," the man said.

"Let's have a drink," a woman's voice cut in. "And forget about this."

"Clive didn't realize Birdie was with you," Boston Bob's voice rang loudly as he tried to calm things down. "But now he does. A drink is a mighty good way of clearing this all up."

I stepped around Mason as Clive nodded in agreement with Boston Bob as he turned his back on Mason.

I was about to head to the bar to get a drink, but Mason's following words stopped me.

"Not you..." He took a step towards Clive Malone.

The woman next to Clive grabbed his arm and pulled him away. "Come on, Whiskey, he meant nothing by it," she said, fluttering her lashes before turning back to Clive. "You still want a job in the morning, right, Clive?"

I stood next to Mason as they went to the far side of the bar. "He works for you?" I asked.

Boston Bob stepped in front of me, blocking the group. "The distillery provides most of Moon's Landing with work. Well, you have a nine out of ten chance of getting it right!" Boston Bob revealed. "But you're in luck. Rascal Ferret isn't here tonight."

"And that's luck?" I asked, confused.

"It's best if you don't get mixed up with someone like Rascal Ferret," Boston Bob mumbled behind his hand.

"It's getting late," Mason said. "Why don't we head home?"

"That's a great idea! Have a great night," Boston Bob waved us off before heading away.

"I'm sure someone here knows how we can find Rascal Ferret," I argued. I wasn't ready to leave.

Mason tilted his head and nodded toward an older man leaning against a bar table. His hair was neatly combed, and he sported a thin mustache above his lip. "Someone does."

As if on cue, the man was heading over to us.

"Mason Moon?" He asked. "Wichita Willie told me to talk to you."

Good ol' Wichita!

"Wichita told me you would keep this between us," he stated hushedly. "I don't want Ferret to know I talked."

"You can trust us," I answered encouragingly. "Do you know how we can find him?"

He nodded and then glanced over his shoulder. "But it's not a 'him' you should look for."

"What do you mean?" I asked, confused.

"She hangs out around here on Sundays. You can always find her near her car. Don't know her real name, just what I told you."

"What kind of car does she drive?" Mason asked.

"It's a Black Sedan with one of those old-fashioned hood ornaments of a Ferret." He cupped his hands together as he tried to describe it. "I heard Kentucky Marv learned who she was. He was boasting about it to me and one of the other guys."

"Well, who is she?" I asked in a rush of excitement, feeling we were getting closer.

"He didn't say," he shrugged. "He only told us he had a meeting with a reporter who he had sold his story. Someone by the initials of T.D."

"T.D.?" I asked. Turning to Mason, I said, "Could he have been talking about Tony Diggs?" We had to find him before Rascal Ferret did. Tony Diggs could be in trouble.

Chapter Twelve

BUTTERSCOTCH AND I WERE UP EARLY AND HEADED out for a walk. We were in the middle of our route when I spotted Vivian Dupont driving down the street. She waved at us, and as I waved back, I couldn't help but wonder what had brought her into our neighborhood.

Vivian pulled her sedan to the side of the road and waved me over. "Birdie," she called. "Good morning."

Butterscotch and I hurried over to her driver's side window. "Good morning." What was all of this about?

Her eyes were hidden behind a pair of dark tortoise sunglasses, and her red lips were set in a straight line. I had the feeling that this wouldn't be a social call.

"I was taking the chance I'd find you at home," she said, her voice soft. I had to strain to hear. "But this works all the same."

Butterscotch swatted her paw against the door. "Oh, no," Vivian sputtered as she exited the car. "Your dog is going to scratch the paint." She hurried to inspect it. She was rubbing her fingers against a streak.

There wasn't a scratch on the shiny black paint, and I told

her as much. "Is there something I can do for you?" I couldn't imagine what she was doing here, but I thought it would be best to be nice to her. Maybe I could convince her to rethink her decision on Blanche's loan. Anything's possible. Vivian must have read my mind because she brought up the loan.

"I feel terrible about turning down Blanche, but you see, she and her father just don't have the right capital, and it would be best if they sold the paper instead of draining more and more money into it." She adjusted the tortoise sunglasses on her head.

"Are you sure?" I asked. "Blanche has an excellent business plan that needs time to develop."

Vivian waved her hand at me and removed her sunglasses, using them to point at me. "I'm not here to be convinced. I just wanted to let you know that I feel terrible for her, but in the end, she will find it was the best decision."

"But the paper is her father's legacy," I argued.

Vivian thinned out her lips as she grimaced at me. "Her father's legacy? I know Henry Pruitt better than you do, and let me tell you, that man doesn't know a thing about what a legacy is." She opened her car door and sat inside, slamming the door shut.

Butterscotch barked in protest, and we jumped back. "This isn't about Blanche. You're unfairly associating your negative feelings towards Henry Pruitt with his daughter."

Her eyes narrowed sharply at me. "Am I?" Vivian sat back in her seat and placed her sunglasses over her eyes. "Then I have nothing more to say to you."

Butterscotch and I jumped back further as Vivian drove away from the curb. I patted Butterscotch on her head to ensure she was alright, and then we continued with our walk. I didn't know if I should tell Blanche what had just happened. She didn't need to hear any more bad news.

It was nearly twenty minutes later when we reached home.

I spotted Mason heading towards his car parked in the drive-way. As I waved to him, Butterscotch barked. Having him live next door while we worked on this case together was convenient.

"Good morning," he said. "I was headed out to work."

"Already? It's barely six thirty."

"I have an early meeting," he explained.

I wanted to ask him if he had thought more about buying Moon's News, but I could see he was in a rush as he opened the driver's door and tossed in a folder.

I would have to talk to him about it later.

It wasn't until after breakfast that I wished I hadn't decided to wait to speak to Mason about buying the newspaper.

* * *

Blanche knocked restlessly at my front door, calling my name as she did so. I had just finished a shower, and my hair was still wet as I answered the door. Blanche rushed inside, sputtering frantically.

"Birdie, you have to come with me," she sobbed.

"Go with you where?" I asked, confused.

"To the bank," she said in a rush before grabbing my purse off the side table. "It closes in an hour. We don't have much time."

"Has something happened? I thought you were turned down for the loan." I couldn't just go with her — my hair is still wet!

Blanche whirled at me with my purse clutched in her arms. Butterscotch barked with excitement as she pranced around Blanche. Blanche adverted her eyes from me as she said, "Well, that's where you come in."

"Me?" I asked. "How do I fit into this?" I asked Butterscotch to calm down as I headed into the kitchen to heat the kettle.

"Can we talk about this in the car?" Blanche pleaded. "I'd love to bring Butterscotch, but I don't believe the banks a good place for her."

Feeling pressed for time, I grabbed a scarf from a drawer by the door, used it to cover my hair, and followed Blanche to the car. "Can you tell me what's happening?" I asked.

"Of course," she said as she glanced. "Absolutely."

But she didn't. She kept me literally on the edge of my seat to the bank. It wasn't until she parked that she finally told me what this was all about. Blanche turned to me, her eyes locked onto mine. I suddenly became worried.

"What is this all about?" I asked.

Blanche took a deep breath before answering. "I need you to co-sign on the loan with me."

"Me?" I gasped. I was not expecting this. "Me?" I asked again, assuming there was more to this explanation. "You want me to co-sign with you?"

"I'm desperate here, Birdie," she cried. "There is no other option. You are it! I can't get Vivian to approve of me — no matter what I promise. You are all dad, and I have left to turn to."

Blanche knew I would do anything for her and her dad, but I had to explain what Vivian Dupont had said. "There's nothing you can do." I didn't want to tell her this, but I felt there was no choice. "That woman will never give you a loan. She as much as told me so earlier today."

"What?" Her jaw dropped, and her eyes widened in shock. "What did you just say?" Blanche clutched her hand to her mouth and trembled in defeat.

I leaned my elbow against the side of the door's paneling and rested my head in my hand. I hated seeing the look of anguish on her face.

Blanche shook her head in denial, and within moments, she was racing out of the car and running at full speed into the bank. I nearly fell over my feet as I rushed to follow her. What is she going to do?

"Blanche," I yelled. As I entered the bank, I spotted her at the door to Vivian Dupont's office. It was too late to stop her from doing whatever it was she got into her mind to do, but I ran to her side. "Blanche?" I grabbed her arm with no intention of letting her go inside that office.

The office is empty, thank goodness! "Blanche, let's get out of here," I said as I tugged her arm toward the door.

Blanche turned to me with tears filling her eyes. "You don't understand," she confided. "The paper is in debt, and my dad is swimming in past due loans that he's unable to repay."

"I'm sure there's something we can do. Maybe try a bank outside of Moon's Landing?"

"Aunt Lula didn't leave you a fortune in the basement, did she?" She asked with a half smile and wiped at her tears.

I opened my purse to give her a tissue and shook my head. There is an option, one that I'm desperate to try. "What about Mason? Maybe he will buy it?"

Blanche shook her head. "And work for him? It would never work. I have my way of doing business, and he would want to run it his way."

"But it would keep the doors open." Mason had talked to me about it and suggested it would be a money pit, but the man's rich! He could afford it. "Come on, let's go grab some coffee."

I crossed my fingers that Mason would make Blanche an offer, one she couldn't refuse. But fate would play another card, and no one saw it coming.

Chapter Thirteen

BLANCHE AND I HEADED TO *SWEETIE'S LATTES* AND found it packed with customers, both locally and from a tour bus. The bus was parked diagonally in the parking lot, which caused us to park one street over. I dropped my bag as we weaved through the parking lot, causing me to stop.

"Oh, no!" I mumbled as I stooped down to retrieve it, but my tube of lipstick jumped out of my purse and rolled away from me. A pair of polished black boots stepped to my left as a gloved hand snatched up the tube of lipstick, causing me to glance up to see who had rescued it.

"Birdie," Lomack said as he handed me the lipstick. "Is this yours?"

I smiled as I grabbed it from him. "Thank you."

He started walking into the Sweeties, but I quickly grabbed his arm and stopped him. "Wait a minute," I said.

"I'm on duty," he said.

"Wait a second," Blanche said, finding her voice. "You took a risk leaving those notes. Thank you."

"All right," he said. Lomack's walkie-talkie beeped as an operator's voice came on the line.

"We got a problem down at the Station," the operator stated.

Lomack lifted the walkie to his mouth, speaking firmly, "I'm headed into Sweeties. Can't Griffins deal with it?"

"Deputy Griffins asked for you."

He responded with a heavy sigh that he'd be at the Station in about twenty minutes.

"What do you suppose that's about?" I asked Blanche.

Blanche's eyes followed Lomack back to his patrol car, a mischievous glimmer in her eyes. "Only one way to find out," she said, grabbing my hand and yanking me towards the car. "The coffee can wait."

Chapter Fourteen

Blanche and I rushed into the Sheriff's Station, hot behind Lomack, who had stormed inside. "What is going on in here?" He demanded.

Deputy Joe Murphy was seated at the front desk, and the radio operator was behind him. Joe cleared his throat, standing before answering. "It's Tennesse Langford, Sir. He was just arrested."

"Tennesse Langford was arrested?" Blanche asked, bewildered. She clamped her hand on my arm, and her face was white as she turned to me. "He's back?"

"Why was he arrested?" Lomack demanded but then shook his head. "It doesn't matter — where do you have him?"

"Griffins has him in holding," Joe answered grimly. He sat down as Lomack hurried into the holding area.

"What is he doing back?" Blanche asked. "Why was he arrested?"

Tennesse Langford was Blanche's ex-fiance. He broke her heart nearly two years ago. With no explanation, he just called off the wedding and was gone. I had hoped Blanche would never have to see him again, but now that he's back, what would that do to Blanche?

Clarice, the radio operator, leaned over Joe's shoulder as though she were about to spill secrets. "He was arrested for destroying public property."

Blanche gasped. "What? Why would he do that?"

"That's what we hope to get to the bottom of," Joe clarified. "Griffins was the one who brought him in. He took a bat to the welcoming sign for Moon's Landing."

Ben Griffins and Tennesse Langford were best friends. Even Griffins had yet to learn what had happened with Tennesse. He had vanished, and everyone had looked at Blanche for being the cause, believing she had broken his heart somehow. Blanche had weathered it, focusing on her work.

Clarice held her hand to her neck, tugging at her necklace. "I heard he's returning to Moon's Landing for good." Her eyes shifted from Blanche to me. "It'll be good to have him back home."

Everyone knew he had left Blanche at the altar. It was all Doris Gilbert would speak about on her blog for weeks.

"Blanche, why don't we head to Moon's News?" I suggested. "We have to work on our case."

"What?" Blanche asked, distracted, as her eyes focused on me. "Yes, let's do that. There's nothing for me here."

I caught Clarice and Joe exchanging a look of pity.

"This couldn't have happened at the worst time," Blanche replied as we returned to the car. "Why is he back here?"

* * *

Beaker was waiting for us at the door to Moon's News. He must have seen Blanche's red convertible pull into the drive.

Blanche took the cup of coffee he had in his hands and took a long drink. "Beaker, you have the look of bad news all over you. What is it? I need a distraction, and it better have nothing to do with Tennesse Langford."

"Tennesse?" He asked, confused. "Why would I bring him up?" He looked at me for an explanation, and I only shrugged, not wanting to talk about him either. I silently followed Blanche to her office.

"Blanche, wait," he called, but he was too late; Blanche had her door open, and who would be sitting in her chair behind her desk?

Tony Diggs. He looked quite at home, and he had a broad smile.

"What are you doing in my chair?" Blanche demanded. "How did you get in here?"

Tony didn't move. Instead, he leaned back and clasped his hands. The last we had heard, he had been released from jail, and Deputy Murphy would round him up to bring him in for questioning.

"I got released. Something about special circumstances, but I'm not allowed to speak about it. I heard you were looking for me," he explained. "I heard you regretted firing me."

"We didn't fire you," she pointed out.

"Budget cuts are the same as being fired," he explained. "But it doesn't matter. I heard I may be offered my old job back."

"Your job?" She asked, stunned. "Where did you hear this?"

He glanced over her shoulder at Beaker, who shrugged. "That's what I wanted to speak to you about." He handed Blanche a folder. "It's about the case you are working on. I might have told him he could have his old job back if he came in."

"Do I have a job or not?" Tony asked. "I heard you needed me."

Blanche crossed her arms. "I do, but it might be dangerous."

Tony leaned forward and placed his elbows on top of the desk. He was intrigued. "In what way?"

"Get us Rascal Ferret," Blanche grinned coyly. "And your old job is yours."

Tony's face fell flat. That wasn't what he was expecting Blanche to say. "How am I supposed to do that?"

"I'll make us some coffee," Beaker stated as he closed the door, closing me in with them.

"Maybe we should explain what this is about," I suggested. I held out my hand to shake his. "Hi, I'm Birdie Lopez." He didn't take my hand, so I awkwardly dropped it and cleared my throat. "We are looking into the murder of Kentucky Marv. I believe you know him well."

"I know him," he said. "We all know what happened to him."

"We?" I inquired.

"The S.O.S.'s," he said.

"You're a member?" I asked. I had thought only janitors were members of the group.

"An honorary member. My father was president for years." He leaned back in the chair. "Do I have my old job back or what?"

"That all depends," Blanche stated firmly. "If I give you your old job back, I need to know if you can deliver on this case."

"You want me to tell you about Rascal Ferret?" He raised his brows and raked his hand through his hair. "Do you have any idea what you're asking of me?"

Blanche nodded. "I do, but we want answers. Kentucky Marv was our janitor here for years. He didn't deserve what happened to him."

"Kentucky Marv was a good man. He was different from

the rest of us." He stood as he retrieved his phone from his back pocket and began typing. "All I can offer you is this."

Blanche's phone pinged. She had received a text message. "What's this?" She asked as she read the message containing an address.

"It's where you can find Rascal Ferret. But don't say where you got it from. Rascal will be there tonight at ten." He pulled his jacket from the coat rack. "I'll be back in the morning and working from my old desk." He pushed past us as he left the office.

"Well," I asked. "Does he have his old job back?"

"Of course he does — but for how long? Unless we get a miracle, we are on the verge of closing our doors."

She was right. It was going to take a miracle to keep the newspaper in business. I got back to the case at hand. "What about the address? Where are we going?"

"It's the address to Bootlegger Bowl."

I peered over her shoulder to read the message. "It has instructions," I said as I read them.

"But they make no sense." She stuck her phone back into her pocket. "Perform the SOS in code? What does that even mean?"

"I can help you with that," I replied with a smile. Are we finally going to find Rascal Ferrett?

Chapter Fifteen

WE ARRIVED AT *BOOTLEGGER BOWL* AN HOUR EARLY, and fortunately, it was a slow night. Only a few lanes were used, and two patrons sat at the bar.

"Not a busy night for someone like Rascal Ferret to be making deals," Blanche remarked as we stood at the entrance.

"Don't worry, I have a hunch things are busy elsewhere in the building," I said as I walked towards the back.

"What are you talking about?" Blanche asked, confused, but followed. "If that man sent us on a wild goose chase, he will find himself out of a job again!"

I moved quickly through the bowling alley, heading straight to the janitor's closet; finding it unlocked, I walked inside.

"What are we doing here?" Blanche asked as she stood outside the door.

"Come in and close the door behind you," I ordered.

Quickly, I moved to the plunger in the sink and turned the handle counterclockwise. Next, I moved to the wall beside the sink and knocked S.O.S. in Morse Code.

"What are you doing?" Blanche asked. "When did you

learn Morse Code?"

"I've been here before, but I'll tell you about it another time." I smiled as the door slid open.

"A secret door?" Blanche asked, bewildered. "Where does this go?"

I glanced over my shoulder as I answered. "To a secret underground society known as the Society of Sanitation." I took her hand and pulled her in behind me. The society was buzzing with action, and no one seemed to notice us, and that was fine with me.

"What is going on in here?" Blanche whispered.

"I'll explain later, but first, let's go to the bar and ask about Rascal Ferret."

Blanche followed me, trying not to gawk at what was happening around us. Fortunately for us, Wichita Willie was bartending. "Good evening," I said with a sly smile.

His eyes grew large as he looked at me. "What are you doing here? I thought you were warned away."

I shook my head and leaned across the bar to confide. "You know who I'm here to see. Is she here?" I was afraid to speak the name, fearing one of the patrons would overhear and warn Rascal Ferret.

"Are you still looking for you know who?" He questioned. "I told you to leave it alone."

"Which one is he?" Blanche asked, scanning the room. "All you have to do is point him out."

Wichita Willie lifted a shaky hand and pointed at three men and one woman standing near the scoreboard. "But it's being handled," he said through gritted teeth.

Blanche didn't wait another moment as she dashed from the bar. "Excuse me," she muttered as she 'accidentally' knocked into the woman in her haste to reach them. Blanche turned to her to apologize again, but this time, she got a better look at the woman. "Vivian? Vivian Dupont?"

I hurried to her side, surprised as she was to find Vivian Dupont here. "Vivian?" I stammered. "What are you doing here?"

Vivian is Rascal Ferret?

Her eyes moved sharply between the two of us. "Are you following me?" She demanded nervously. "Never mind," she pushed between us to leave, but Blanche held out her arm, blocking her path.

"Wait a minute," Blanche said. "Are you Rascal Ferret?"

"Rascal, who?" Vivan asked, confusion lighting up her face. "Excuse me, but I don't have time for this. Let me pass."

"Just a minute." Blanche stepped in front of her and crossed her arms in defiance. "You've got to explain to me why everyone here believes you're Rascal—"

"Stop calling me by that name," Vivian spat furiously. "Now let me pass, or I will—"

"You'll what?" Blanche wasn't backing down.

Wichita Willie pointed her out as the infamous Rascal Ferret, so unless he's confused — which I highly doubt. Vivian must be the one we're looking for.

"Rascal Ferret!" Boston Bob called out her name. He stormed over and towered over her. "What are you doing back here?"

Vivian knocked Boston Bob aside with her bag as she ran out.

I didn't hesitate; I ran after her. "Vivian, wait!"

Blanche and I followed her into the parking lot, where Vivian was quick to pull a gun out of her bag. "Not another step," she yelled.

Boston Bob nearly knocked me over as I stopped. "She's got a gun," I shouted. I didn't move. "Vivian, think about what you are doing."

She shook her head. "Why are the two of you following me?"

"We know you shot Kentucky Marv," Blanche explained.

I shook my head as I calmly stated, "But I'm sure it was an accident." I wanted to keep her calm. *She's holding a gun at us.* "You didn't mean to shoot Kentucky Marv, did you?"

Vivian pointed the gun directly at me. "How would you know what I meant to do or not?"

"You didn't mean to hurt him." I had to keep her talking because I had hoped that someone from inside would call Lomack.

"It was an accident," Vivian stated as she vigorously nodded. "I only brought the gun for protection. But he made me so mad when he told me he wouldn't pay me what he owed, and instead, he had the gall to blackmail me. Me!"

Blanche took a step forward, causing Vivian to turn the gun on her. "Kentucky Marv was scared," Blanche stated. "But why not give him more time than shoot him?"

"I needed my money! The bank was sending an auditor. They would have found out the money was missing. The money I was using as —"

"So you shot him?" Blanche took a step forward.

"Blanche, wait," I shouted. What is she going to do?

Slowly, Blanche reached out her hand, holding it out for the weapon. "Why don't you give me that? I'll help you."

Vivian took a step back, shaking her head. "*You* want to help me? I don't need you to help me." She took another step back.

"Vivian, you're in a lot of trouble," Blanche reminded. "You murdered Kentucky Marv!"

"But I didn't mean to," she waved the gun back and forth between me and Blanche. "But he told me he had already spoken to his friend who worked at the newspaper. Everything about me was going to come out."

I shook my head. "He never got the chance to speak to anyone."

"What?" Vivian swung the gun back at me. Her eyes grew wide with shock. "But he told me. He told me it was a done deal."

I hadn't noticed, but Boston Bob had slowly moved around us to come up behind Vivian. She was so focused on Blanche and me that she hadn't seen his movements. Boston Bob launched himself onto Vivian, wrapping a bulky arm around her shoulder while also reaching for the gun.

The gun fired a round. I heard the bullet sizzle by me, and I ducked down behind a car. "Blanche," I shrieked. "Are you okay?"

"Birdie," she called back. "I'm okay — are you okay?"

"Yes!" Carefully, I glanced up from behind the car. Boston Bob had secured Vivian in his arms, and the gun lay several feet away. Blanche hurried to retrieve it. The sound of police sirens railed in the distance.

I spotted Mason jumping out of his car and running to us. "What happened?"

"What are you doing here? Never mind, I'll fill you in over coffee," I said as I dusted myself off, relieved it was over. I spared a glance at him and found his shirt covered in a red stain. "What's on your shirt?"

Mason glanced down at his button-up shirt and wiped a hand over it. "I was at the brewery," he said, as if that would explain its condition.

"Is that blood on your shirt?" I asked, pointing at it in confusion.

"Blood?" Blanche asked as she joined us. She was still holding the gun but pointed downward. "Don't be silly, Birdie. Why would Mason have blood on his shirt..." her eyes widened as she realized it may indeed be blood. "What happened?"

"I'm not going to have time to explain," he said.

But the nearing sirens were deafening, and I didn't think I

could hear if he had explained.

"But coffee will have to wait," he explained. "I'm going to be arrested."

"What?" I shouted.

"Mr. Moon?" Griffins called out as he stepped out of his patrol car. "I'm going to need you to come to the station…"

"What?" I asked, confused. "Why?"

The look on Mason's face was severe, and it caused me to become concerned. "What is this all about?"

Mason grinned. "Wichita Willie called me, and I rushed right down here, but I may have caused a police chase…" he glanced over at Deputy Griffins.

"A what?" I asked, confused.

Boston Bob spoke with Deputy Murphy as Vivian was being loaded into the patrol car, and Blanche handed the gun to Griffins. But Mason had my attention.

"There's been a murder at the brewery," he said, his voice low.

"A murder?" I couldn't believe it. Another murder?

Griffins stood behind Mason, his hands on his hips as he waited. "Mr. Moon?"

"But why are you being arrested?" I asked as I saw the handcuffs in Griffins' hand.

Mason gave me a half smile, took my hands, and leaned close to me. His gray eyes were clear and steady as they looked into mine. He dropped a pair of keys in my hand before turning to Griffins, who promptly placed Mason under arrest.

Murder? Griffins stated Mason was being arrested for murder… I hurried to Blanche who was speaking to Boston Bob. "Blanche," I said as I grabbed her. "We need to go — now."

"What?" she asked. "I'm busy at the moment. I'm conducting interviews. I can't just leave."

I shook my head. "Mason's just been arrested!"

Thank you for reading my book!

If you enjoyed Murder by Copy, I would love it if you let your friends know and leave me a review. Reviews will help other readers discover my book! :)

Thank you!
Shelley

About the Author

Shelley Weiss is a dreamer of all things magical. She loves to write poems and drink coffee. When she's not writing, she's working on her endless sewing projects and reading books. She and her husband live in Southern California with their menagerie of pets.

If you wish to be notified about her next book or giveaway, sign up for her mailing list at
https://mailchi.mp/a4b922a81b38/newsletter

* 9 7 9 8 2 2 4 7 9 3 5 0 1 *